P9-DXN-720

To Katie and Ben.
—D.L.

Clarion Books
3 Park Avenue
New York, New York 10016

Copyright © 2015 by David Litchfield

First published in the U.K. in 2015 by Frances Lincoln Children's Books,
74-77 White Lion Street, London N19PF.

Published in the U.S. in 2016.

All rights reserved. For information about permission to reproduce selections from this book,
write to trade.permissions@hmhco.com or to Permissions,
Houghton Mifflin Harcourt Publishing Company,
3 Park Avenue, 19th Floor, New York, New York 10016.

Clarion Books is an imprint of Houghton Mifflin Harcourt Publishing Company.

www.hmhco.com

The illustrations in this book were done in mixed media.
The text was set in Granjon LT.

Library of Congress Cataloging-in-Publication Data
Names: Litchfield, David.
Title: The bear and the piano / by David Litchfield.
Description: Boston ; New York : Clarion Books, Houghton Mifflin Harcourt, [2016] | Summary:
"A bear finds a piano in the woods, learns to play it, and travels to the big city to become rich and famous,
but ultimately discovers that his old friends in the forest back home are still the best audience of all."
—Provided by publisher.
Identifiers: LCCN 2015020008 | ISBN 9780544674547 (hardback)
Subjects: | CYAC: Bears—Fiction. | Piano—Fiction. | Music—Fiction. | Friendship—Fiction. | BISAC: JUVENILE
FICTION / Animals / Bears. | JUVENILE FICTION / Imagination & Play. | JUVENILE FICTION / Performing
Arts / Music. | JUVENILE FICTION / Social Issues / Friendship.
Classification: LCC PZ7.1.L575 Be 2016 | DDC [E]—dc23
LC record available at http://lccn.loc.gov/2015020008

Manufactured in China
10 9 8 7 6 5 4 3 2
4500575085

The Bear
and the
Piano

WITHDRAWN

BY David Litchfield

CLARION BOOKS
Houghton Mifflin Harcourt
Boston   New York

One day in the forest, a young bear cub found something he'd never seen before.

What could this strange thing be? he thought. Shyly, he touched it with his stubby paws.

PLONK!

The strange thing made an
awful sound.

So the bear left.

But the next day he came back,

and the day after that, too.

And for days and weeks and months and years,

until eventually…

. . . the sounds that came from the strange
thing were beautiful, and the bear had grown
big and strong and grizzly.

When the bear played, he felt so happy.

The sounds took him away from the forest,

and he dreamed of strange and wonderful lands.

It wasn't long before the other bears
in the forest were drawn to the clearing.

Every night, a crowd gathered to listen
to the magical melodies coming from
the bear and the strange thing.

Then, one night, a girl and her father came across the clearing.

They told the bear that the strange thing was a piano and the sounds it made were music.

"Come to the city with us," they said. "There is lots of music there. You can play grand pianos in front of hundreds of people and hear sounds so beautiful they will make your fur stand on end."

The bear knew that if he left the forest, the other bears would be very sad.

But he longed to explore the world beyond
the woods, to hear more wonderful music,
and to play bigger and better than before.

And before long . . .

. . . the bear's name was up in big,
bright lights in the big, bright city.

"UN MISSABLE!"

ONE WAY

W 58 ST

BROADWAY

THE POST
YOU WON'T
BELIEVE
YOUR
EARS
OR YOUR
EYES!!!

He played sold-out concerts

in giant theaters.

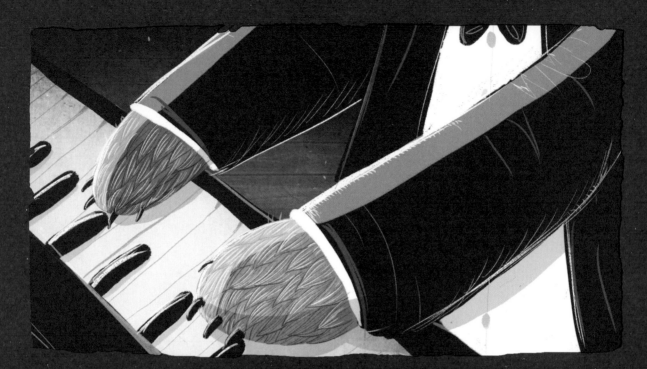

Every night, he performed

with such passion

and such grace,

to wild applause

and standing ovations

and huge admiration.

The bear recorded albums that went platinum.
He was interviewed for magazines.
He won awards.
He met new people every day.
And created headlines everywhere he went.

The city was everything he had hoped it would be.

But deep down, something tugged at the bear's heart.

He had fame and awards and all the music in the world,
but he missed the forest.

He missed his old friends.

He missed his home.

So the bear decided to go back.
He speedily crossed the river . . .

. . . and excitedly pounded into the forest. He couldn't
wait to tell his friends about his time in the city.

But when the bear reached the
familiar clearing, it was empty.

No piano, no bears, no anything.

The bear started to worry that his friends had forgotten him, or that they were angry that he had left them behind.

Then a friend stepped into the clearing.
"Hello!" cried the bear. "I'm back.
I've missed you so much!"

Without saying a word, the gray bear ran back into the trees.
   "Wait!" called the bear. "I'm sorry I left. Please stop!"
But his friend just kept running.

The bear stumbled after him, moving deeper
and deeper into the forest,

until he saw something that made his fur stand on end.

For the bear had not been forgotten.
His friends weren't angry, but proud.

The bear realized that no matter where he went, or what he did,
they would always be there, watching from afar.

They had even kept the piano safe
in the shade, ready for his return.

So after the bear had told his
friends about his life in the city,
and the many concerts he had played,
he sat down to play once more.

This time, for the most
important audience of all.

CONTRA COSTA COUNTY LIBRARY

31901059200701